VIKING
Published by the Penguin Group
Viking Penguin, a division of Penguin Books USA Inc.,
375 Hudson Street, New York, New York 10014, U.S.A.
Penguin Books Ltd, 27 Wrights Lane, London W8 5TZ, England
Penguin Books Australia Ltd, Ringwood, Victoria, Australia
Penguin Books Canada Ltd, 2801 John Street, Markham, Ontario, Canada L3R 1B4
Penguin Books (N.Z.) Ltd, 182–190 Wairau Road, Auckland 10, New Zealand

Penguin Books Ltd, Registered Offices: Harmondsworth, Middlesex, England

First published in Switzerland by bohem press, 1988
First American edition published in 1991
1 3 5 7 9 10 8 6 4 2
Copyright © bohem press, 1988
All rights reserved
ISBN 0-670-83677-X
Library of Congress catalog card number: 90-70732

Printed in Italy
Set in Ronda Light

Bob
the Snowman

Sylvia Loretan · Jan Lenica

Viking

It had been snowing all day and all the children in the neighborhood were busy building a beautiful snowman. When they finished, they named him Bob. They put a broom in his hand and an old hat on his head.

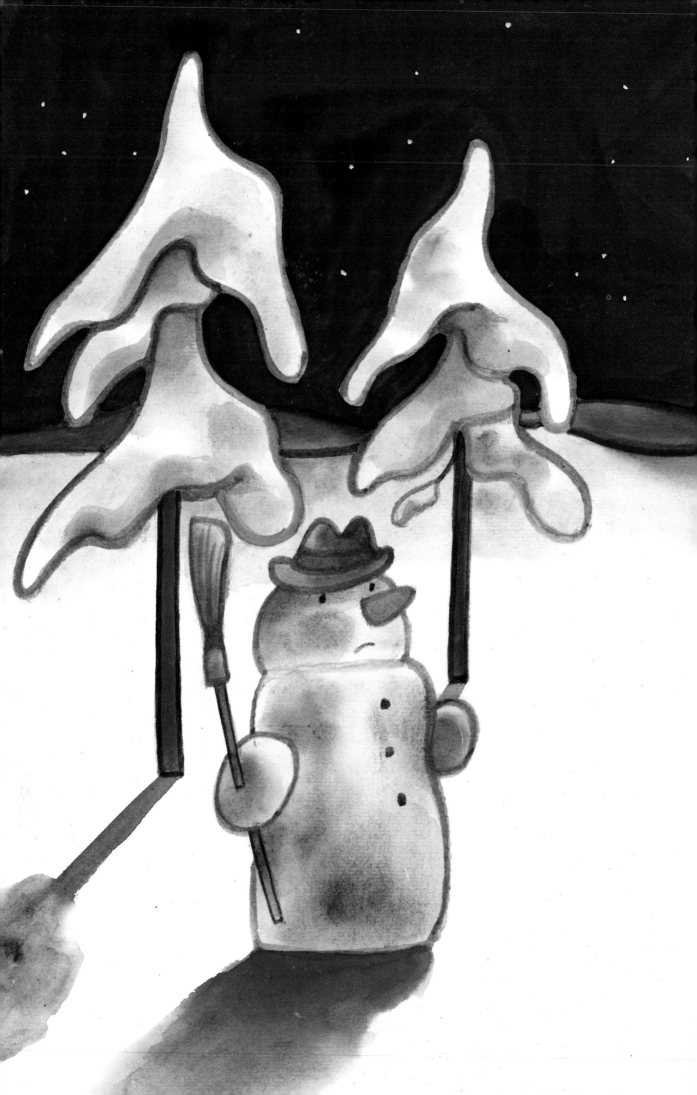

Bob was happy. He liked everything, especially the
children who were having so much fun around him.

When it got dark, the children went home. Bob was
all lonely.

Suddenly a bird appeared. He sat on a tree and shook his wings. "Brrr . . ." he said, "it's too cold here. I'm on my way south. All my friends have left already, and I'm late. In the south, we will eat fruit off the trees, and sing beautiful songs." Then he stretched his wings and flew off into the dark night.

All night long, Bob thought about what the bird had told him. He dreamt about this beautiful, faraway country. He imagined himself on the beach, standing under a palm tree, with a snow-woman at his side, listening to the birds' songs. With his broom he would wave to the passing boats. He liked that idea.

Suddenly Bob decided to go south, too.

At dawn, Bob walked to the train station. He thought of the children and he felt sad. They would miss him! As he walked, he began to sweat. His carrot nose began to quiver and his hat slipped down on his head.

The train was already waiting when Bob arrived at the station. He saw a lot of people getting on and off the train, but he didn't see any other snowmen.

Then a voice shouted, "All aboard!" So Bob climbed
onto the luggage car and the door was shut.

Inside, it was dark and scary. Bob couldn't see anything. The only sound was the clackety-clack of the wheels. Then Bob started getting warmer and warmer. He was sweating a lot. Bob became smaller and smaller. Suddenly his hat slipped off his head! Then he lost an eye, then his carrot nose. Bob was worried. He was getting so small that you could hardly see him.

By the time the train arrived in the south, Bob had turned into a puddle!

"Oh, dear," Bob thought, "now that I am a puddle, what
will happen to me?" Sunbeams called to him, "Come on,

climb up!" So drop by drop, Bob climbed up into the sky,
where he turned into a soft, white cloud.

Then a strong wind blew Bob and the other clouds over the land. It was a wonderful flight. Exactly above the children's

neighborhood, Bob came to a rest. As it grew colder, Bob
turned into snowflakes.

"Hooray! It's snowing!" cried the children. "Let's build a
new Bob!" And they built a beautiful new snowman.
Now Bob could laugh again. He was happy to be back
and to be a snowman once more.

He never wanted to travel again. The next morning, the
children were very glad to see that Bob was still there.
And they built a whole family for him.

Only Bob knew that one day the snow family would all become puddles again. But he was not sad. He knew they would all climb into a cloud and wait for next winter.